THE ICONIUM MYSTERY

OVERTAKING THE MEN

Page 38   *Frontispiece*

THE
ICONIUM MYSTERY

BY

JOHN MAURICE

With frontispiece by
ROBERT JOHNSTON

BLACKIE & SON LIMITED
LONDON AND GLASGOW

BLACKIE & SON LIMITED
16/18 William IV Street,
Charing Cross, London, W.C.2
17 Stanhope Street, Glasgow

BLACKIE & SON (INDIA) LIMITED
103/5 Fort Street, Bombay

BLACKIE & SON (CANADA) LIMITED
Toronto

Printed in Great Britain by Blackie & Son, Ltd., Glasgow

CONTENTS

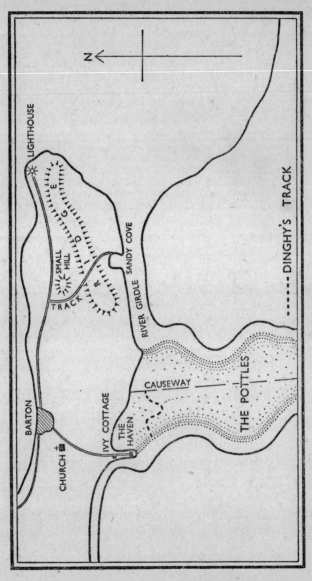

THE HAVEN AND ITS SURROUNDINGS

------ DINGHY'S TRACK

THE ICONIUM MYSTERY

Chapter I   *The Haven*

"JOHN, are you quite sure that you and Peter will be all right here on your own?" asked Mrs. Pencastle.

"Quite," said John firmly.

"There are only another five days of the holidays, so you'll be home soon. I have made a list of the food which you'll want," added Mrs. Pencastle, regarding her son with a sudden access of maternal anxiety.

"We'll be all right, Mother," said John.

"Well, the taxi's here. I suppose that we'd better be off. Good-bye, John. Good-bye, Peter. Do be careful!"

"She's a jolly good mother, but women do fuss so," remarked John to his friend Peter Fennel as they waved good-bye to the departing taxi. "Does your mother fuss?"

"Sometimes. It's going to be jolly good fun having the cottage and the boat to ourselves," said Peter, grinning cheerfully.

The Pencastle family were in the habit of taking

a cottage for their summer holidays. This year they had chosen one by the banks of the River Girdle. It had been built by a retired master mariner, who had called it " The Haven ". The name was well chosen, for the cottage, though small, was well fitted and comfortable.

For the last three weeks of the holidays, the family had been joined by Peter Fennel, John's companion in many adventures. John's father had been compelled to return home before his family, and he was the cause of the sudden departure of Mrs. Pencastle. He had skidded while bicycling on a wet day and had broken his collar-bone. Mrs. Pencastle had hurried home to look after him, taking John's young sister with her. The boys, not entirely to their regret, had been left by themselves.

The country through which the River Girdle ran was generally flat and open. Just below the cottage the river took a tremendous bend to the southward. In the V of the bend was a mass of islands and mudflats, separated by innumerable channels and tidal creeks: this area was known as the Pottles. Beyond the Pottles the river joined the sea.

The Haven itself was very isolated. The old seaman had said that he wanted peace and quiet when he retired. To ensure this he had built his cottage at the end of a peninsula of land with the river on one side and the Pottles on the other. The only approach was by a bumpy road down the peninsula from the village of Barton, some three miles away. With the exception of one cottage at the base of the peninsula, there was not another house in sight.

As the last eddies of dust from the departing taxi dispersed, the boys turned to the river. The sun was shining on the water, the surface of which was ruffled by a light breeze. The whole day was before them and life looked very good indeed.

But the reason did not lie entirely on the weather or the scenery. The garden of The Haven ran down to the river and the garden path continued into the river as a stone pier. Lying off the pier at her moorings was a sixteen-foot, centre-board dinghy. They had taken the boat over with the house and it was the joy of John's heart.

John had sailed boats from his early youth and was capable of handling the dinghy under any conditions. Peter had been bitten by his enthusiasm, and was learning rapidly.

" What about a sail now?" asked Peter.

John looked at the boat doubtfully. The conditions were perfect for a sail. " We've got to go to Barton some time to get food," he said. " What about getting it over this morning and sailing this afternoon? We'll go on our bikes."

" Righto," Peter replied. " Let's have a look at the list."

John pulled the list, which his mother had thrust into his hands before she left, out of his pocket. The two boys studied it in silence.

" There seems to be an awful lot of bread," said John.

" I'm sure that we'll never want all that. I vote that we buy some ginger-beer instead."

John agreed and they set out. They had gone

about half a mile when they saw another bicyclist ahead of them, a woman. She was wobbling all over the road in a most inexpert manner. As they approached she got off, and they saw her examining her back wheel.

"It's Miss Stiggins," said John. "I'll bet she's got a puncture."

"Who's Miss Stiggins?" Peter asked.

"She lives at the cottage we can see from The Haven. It's called Ivy Cottage, I think."

He had no time to say any more for they were close to Miss Stiggins, who was waving frantically.

Miss Stiggins's life appeared to consist of a series of minor crises, but this did not prevent her from exuding friendliness and good nature on every occasion, appropriate or inappropriate.

She was about fifty. Her clothes were of the most nondescript nature and had been flung on in a hurry. The hat obviously had been inherited from an aunt. Behind her large round glasses her eyes shone with enthusiasm, and her lips were permanently parted in a toothy smile.

"Dear boys!" she cooed as they dismounted. "Could you help me? Something seems to be wrong with my back wheel. I'm so stupid about machines."

As the back tyre was completely flat, it was not very difficult to see what was wrong with the back wheel. John stooped down to examine it, while Miss Stiggins fussed round making futile suggestions.

"I was so glad to see you, dear boys," she said. "I saw the taxi leaving The Haven this morning and I thought that you all must have gone."

Peter explained what had happened.

"And you two boys are all on your own!" Her eyes took on an extra gleam of benevolence. "Now if you want a button sewn on, you must bring it to Ivy Cottage. That is one of the things that we women can do." She gave a self-conscious little giggle.

By this time John had discovered that the cause of the trouble was a leaky valve, owing to it not having been screwed home properly. He remedied the trouble and pumped up the tyre.

Miss Stiggins thanked them profusely. "No, don't you dear boys wait for me. I go so slowly. I'll be all right now."

Thankfully the boys rode on, and soon Miss Stiggins was out of sight, still tacking to and fro across the road.

"Phew!" gasped Peter. "Dear boys!"

"I suppose that she means well, though I vote that we manage with our buttons ourselves. Come on. I'll race you to the next corner."

The church at Barton stood some distance outside the village. It was as they were passing it on their way home that Peter suddenly stopped and said, "Gosh!"

"What's the matter?" John asked. "Puncture?"

"No, I'd almost forgotten. Our vicar at home, who's a decent old stick, when he heard that I was going to Barton, asked me to copy out the inscription on a memorial. He's writing a book or something. Do you mind if we go in now?"

The church was open and the boys had little difficulty in finding the memorial. While Peter copied the inscription into his diary, John wandered round the church. Ecclesiastical architecture was not one of John's weaknesses, and he soon found himself examining the Bible open on the lectern.

"They read very curious lessons here," he remarked to Peter when the latter joined him. "We had this one half-way through last term. I remember it quite well because the prefect reading it got all mixed up with the names."

Peter looked at the Bible. It was open at the fourteenth chapter of the Acts of the Apostles.

"And it came to pass in Iconium——"

" I WONDER why sausages always taste so jolly good when you've cooked them yourself," remarked John, as he lay on his back in the sun, digesting his lunch.

" I'm not certain that they always do when I've cooked them," replied Peter with an unexpected burst of modesty.

John sat up and looked at Peter to see if he was displaying any other unusual symptoms. He appeared quite normal.

" We'd better get cracking," John said. " Let's see, high water is at five. And the wind "—he stood up and looked at the direction of the ripples on the surface of the water—" still nor'westerly. I suggest that we run downstream against the tide with the wind astern. At four we'll turn round and beat back with the last of the flood to help us."

" O.K.," said Peter. " It suits me."

Twenty minutes later the dinghy was slipping downstream with a brisk breeze behind her. Peter was steering during this part of the trip, so that John could take her during the more difficult beat back.

The tide was still running quite strongly and,

though the boat was moving fast through the water, progress downstream was slow.

"What about trying to get right through the Pottles and back into the river again?" asked Peter, as they passed the end of an island and could see down an inviting-looking creek leading into the heart of the Pottles.

"I didn't think that we could," John replied. "You remember that causeway that we found on the picnic last week? I think that it goes to the big island at the southern tip. We could never get across that."

"Pity," said Peter, and for a considerable period the only sounds were those of the boat moving through the water and some distant gulls squabbling over some refuse.

John was the first to break the silence.

"Pete, do you sometimes wish that something exciting would turn up, like the adventures that we had before?"

"I don't think so. This is good enough for me." With a wave of his hand Peter included the sunshine, the river and the boat.

There was another long peaceful silence. It struck John, watching the banks, that these were slipping past considerably faster than they had been, although the wind did not appear to have freshened.

"What's the time, Pete?"

"Quarter past three."

"But it was that ages ago."

Peter looked at his watch again. "Gosh, it's stopped! I must have forgotten to wind it up last night."

16   (e 781)

"We'd better turn back now. Bring her up into the wind." John put a hand on the tiller. "I'll take a spell now. No wonder we seemed to be getting on so well."

With John at the tiller and the sheets hauled aft, the boat surged along on the starboard tack, beating up river against the wind.

"I always think that it is silly that a rope controlling the set of a sail should be called a sheet," said Peter. "At first I always thought that you meant the sail, when you told me to haul on the sheet."

"Someone told me that they have been using the word for over a thousand years, so it's a bit late to start complaining now."

John's attention was only partly devoted to Peter's excursions into the realms of philology. He was watching the bank. Instead of being carried upstream by the tide as he had expected, the boat appeared to be making her course.

"Looks as if it's slack water already. That means that we'll have the ebb tide against us most of the way back. Let's hope that the wind holds."

"Sorry about the watch," said Peter.

"It doesn't matter. I expect that we'll be pretty late having supper, though. Just as well Mother's gone. She'd probably be firing rockets and calling out the lifeboat."

This was a gross libel on Mrs. Pencastle, who remained remarkably calm during her son's adventures.

For a while the boys made good progress tacking to and fro across the river. But as the strength of the ebb tide increased, the distance gained on each tack grew less and less. Added to this, the wind began to fail.

"We're barely holding our own," said Peter as, for the third time, they went about close to the same tree.

It was true. The boat was barely moving through the water and at times the sails flapped idly. The Haven was not even in sight.

"Yes, it looks as if we've had it until the tide turns. We'd better make fast to something or we'll be carried right downstream."

John looked round for something suitable. The water alongside the banks was shallow and, with the falling tide, the dinghy would have been left high and dry if they had made fast to a tree.

"What about that stake?" asked Peter, pointing to one of the stakes marking the channel.

"O.K. if we can make it," John grunted, for the tide was now carrying the dinghy downstream.

The boat's progress across the stream was desperately slow and it looked as if they would be carried past the stake. At the last moment a final puff from the dying wind gave the boat just sufficient way to enable Peter to get hold of the stake and secure the dinghy to it with a turn of the painter. It was a good solid stake and the boys had time to take stock of the situation.

"How long do we stay here?" Peter asked.

"I suppose until the tide turns about eleven o'clock."

"It's a pity," remarked Peter after a short pause.

"What's a pity?"

"I was thinking about those two sausages which we left at lunch. I could do with them now."

"So could I. I believe that there are some biscuits in the boat's bag. Let's see." John rummaged in the canvas bag.

He was lucky. There were some rather battered biscuits in a paper bag. They were soft and tasted vaguely of tar, but they were eatable.

As the sun began sinking in the west the scene was one which would have delighted a painter. The flaming reds and yellows of the sky were reflected in the placid water. On the trees the leaves hung motionless. The rooks were indulging in a final burst of noise before retiring to rest. Over the whole area rested an air of deep peace. It was wasted on the boys; they were hungry and rather cold.

The light faded slowly and soon the biscuits were only a pleasant memory. Both boys were becoming very bored when the silence of the evening was disturbed by the distant thud of an engine.

The boys turned and looked downstream. Over one of the low islands they could see the tops of the sails of the yacht, though her hull was still invisible round the bend. The sails were flapping and it was clear that she was making her way upstream on her engine.

"A tow," said Peter in a hopeful voice; "perhaps they'll give us a tow."

Soon the yacht appeared round the bend. She was a ketch of about seven tons. One man was at the tiller and the other was lowering the mizzen.

She was only making slow progress against the tide but she came steadily on.

When she was about a hundred yards away John made a funnel of his hands and holloaed. " Could you give us a tow, please?"

The man at the tiller of the yacht raised his hand in reply and altered course towards them. The other man, an immense man in a blue jersey, picked up a coil of rope, ready to pass it into them as a tow rope.

Suddenly Peter gave a shout, "It's Uncle George!"

The man at the tiller laughed. " I thought that it might be you two scalliwags, but I couldn't be certain in this light. Catch hold of this rope."

The big man threw the rope expertly into the dinghy and soon they were towing comfortably astern towards home.

IT was well after ten when the four of them sat comfortably back in the sitting-room of The Haven with a good supper inside them. The oil lamp—The Haven did not boast of electric light—shed a warm yellow glow over the room. The *Fulmar*, Uncle George's yacht, lay at anchor in the river.

The boys gazed expectantly at Peter's Uncle George; experience had taught them that his visits were usually the forerunner of something exciting.

In appearance he was remarkably undistinguished. As Peter often remarked, it was very difficult to describe Uncle George. He was somewhere in the forties, of medium height with light brown hair, which was just beginning to go thin on top. His face was tanned by exposure to the weather and his eyes sometimes looked blue and sometimes grey. Apart from this it was hard to say anything about his features; they seemed to alter.

His favourite pursuit was bird-watching, but the boys had realized that he had other and more important work; work which had some mysterious connection with the Admiralty.

The fourth member of the party had been introduced as Mr. Baxter.

"And you'd better not get on the wrong side of him," added Uncle George. "He was heavyweight champion of the Mediterranean Fleet in his younger days."

Mr. Baxter was an extremely silent man. At present he was puffing at a pipe with an expression of deep contentment. The pipe emitted clouds of smoke and sinister bubbling noises, so that John felt that it might burst into eruption like a volcano at any moment.

"Well, that's all our news," said John.

Uncle George blew out a cloud of cigarette smoke in a reflective manner. John always felt that it would be more in keeping with his character if he smoked exotic Turkish cigarettes in a long amber holder. Actually he smoked a very common brand of cigarette in a very normal manner.

"I did come here partly with the idea of seeing you, but now that you are on your own, it makes things easier." Uncle George paused and gazed reflectively at the ceiling. "Do you know anything about atomic physics?" he asked.

"We did something about Boy's Law—or was it Boyle's?—in science last term," said Peter cautiously.

"Do you mean about atomic bombs?" John broke in. "Because we had some professor down who gave us a lecture. It was jolly interesting."

"I do," said Uncle George. "My own science is pretty rusty and I don't understand much about it myself. You know that the special uranium they use is very hard to separate out?"

"They have to use a ton of ordinary uranium to

get an ounce of the special stuff, or something like that," John added eagerly.

"I won't dispute your figures, but anyhow it's very difficult to get. Hydrogen also has apparently grave disadvantages. Now"—Uncle George's voice grew very serious—"what I'm going to tell you is strictly between ourselves. I must tell you if you are to help me, but this is strictly Top Secret."

"We promise to keep it to ourselves," said the two boys almost simultaneously. Peter's eyes appeared to be popping out of his head. John wondered if his were doing the same.

"Our scientists have produced a new substance which is just as good as uranium for making bombs and has one great advantage. It has taken them several years to isolate, but once you have a certain amount of it, it is much easier to make more."

"How on earth does that happen?" asked Peter.

"I have no idea," said Uncle George, laughing. "One of the scientists tried to explain, but I only followed the first two sentences. After that I kept on nodding my head and trying to look intelligent."

"But how does this affect us?" asked Peter.

"Because"—Uncle George suddenly became grave once more—"some of the stuff has disappeared. I told you that once you have some of it, it's comparatively easy to make more. So, if once some of the stuff leaves the country and gets into the wrong hands, we will have lost the advantage of all the years of work."

"But surely," John said, "it would be fairly easy to smuggle out a small amount."

" Fortunately not. Being radioactive, it must be kept in a heavy container, and so it's not the sort of thing that you can slip into a suitcase with a false bottom, or the tank of a motor car. It's far more likely that they will try to get it out by boat or possibly aircraft."

" And you think that they may try from round here? Gosh, I'm glad that John asked me to stay." Peter was bubbling over with excitement.

" I do. I won't go into all the reasons why we suspect this area. There is one in particular. Some-one round here has been using a short-wave wireless transmitter, so Baxter and I have come to investi-gate."

" Is there anyone you suspect?" John asked.

" No, that is the trouble. None of the regular people seem to be involved. Of course for a really big job like this they would very likely use a special team. Our friends abroad are very painstaking. They are quite capable of keeping someone doing nothing for five or six years, so that he would be available for an occasion like this without arousing any suspicion."

" Then how do we start?" John was all for setting off that night. " Surely they won't be wandering about carrying large chunks of lead."

" No," replied Uncle George. " There is not much use looking for lead containers. The two lines we have to work on are the wireless signals and the craft coming to collect the stuff. I doubt very much if they would risk an aircraft, and anyhow, that pos-sibility is being taken care of elsewhere. Baxter and

I will go round the coast to find out what chances it offers for a boat to come in without being spotted. Your job is to find out about the wireless signals."

" But——" both boys began.

Uncle George raised his hand. " I know. But how? The chances are that they will have a portable set and will transmit from different places, so as to avoid the risk of being discovered by D/F."

" Direction Finding," whispered John to Peter.

" There are bound to be a lot of visitors round Barton. If any of them are addicted to wandering about the moors carrying something—a short-wave set will go in a suitcase—it might give us a line. That can start to-morrow. And now," looking at the clock, " it's time we all turned in."

" There's just one thing which you haven't told us," said Peter. " What do we call this stuff? It must have a name."

" It has, a lot of letters and figures which would convey nothing to you, even if I could remember them, which I can't. However, they have given it a code name which we will use among ourselves. It's called ' Iconium '."

THE boys were awoken by the arrival of Uncle
George and Mr. Baxter from the *Fulmar*, where
they had slept. It had been agreed that they should
make use of the more spacious cooking arrangements
of The Haven for their meals. Uncle George had
explained that cooking over an oil stove in a tiny
cabin palled very rapidly, though the boys had regarded this with some scepticism.

During breakfast they settled their plans for the
day. The boys would set off for Barton immediately
after the meal on their bicycles. Uncle George and
Mr. Baxter would follow on foot.

" We'll want some form of transport," said Uncle
George. " We'll hire a couple of bicycles in Barton.
It might be fairer to the bicycle if Baxter had a trial
run on his first. I feel that he'll need a fairly stout
one."

" It's over twenty years since I rode one of those
things," retorted Mr. Baxter with a grunt, " but I
reckon that I'll still manage all right."

Uncle George and Mr. Baxter would return to
The Haven on the bicycles and spend the day
examining the coastline in the *Fulmar.* Before dark
they would return to The Haven to meet the boys

and find out if they had any information about suspicious characters.

It was a lovely sunny day as the boys set out and they felt full of optimism in their search. Miss Stiggins was weeding in the garden of Ivy Cottage and waved to them as they passed.

" I suppose that it may have been just a coincidence, as Uncle thought, about the Bible being open at the lesson about Iconium," remarked Peter as they approached the church, " but it was funny, wasn't it?"

" Very," John agreed. " Peter, had you thought exactly how we are going to start looking?"

" No. I hadn't really. Have you any ideas?"

" Well," said John, wrinkling his forehead as was his habit when he was thinking deeply, " I suppose that it will be a man, and if he's not a real holiday-maker, he'll be rather hanging about."

" And that he might be carrying his wireless set in a suitcase. It would be pretty heavy, I suppose."

" He might. It's not very much to go on, is it?"

" No," replied Peter rather uncertainly.

In both boys the early optimism of the morning was ebbing. They realized that they had a difficult job ahead.

Barton had been a thriving port in the Middle Ages, shipping wool to Flanders. Later the trade had begun to decline, and when, some three hundred years ago, the River Girdle had altered its course after disastrous floods and made a new mouth some ten miles from Barton, the port fell into decay. The harbour silted up, and for two hundred years Barton remained a sleepy village with a splendid past.

At the end of the nineteenth century an enterprising contractor had started to develop it as a seaside resort. His grandiose ideas had never been carried out in full, but a considerable number of visitors came each year, attracted by the old-world charm of the place and the excellent bathing. Near the beach was a large hotel which boasted waiters with white shirt-fronts and three stars in the A.A. book.

At the end of two hours' wandering round the beach, both boys were definitely dispirited. Barton seemed to be inhabited by large family parties, and the boys felt that even the most resolute agent would be unlikely to handicap himself by bringing several small children with him.

The streets behind the beach seemed to offer a more hopeful prospect. They were narrow and winding with houses jutting out over the roadway, an ideal place for dark and sinister conspiracy.

"Look!" said John suddenly. "There's a man carrying a heavy case. Let's follow him."

The man had long black hair and looked slightly foreign. He walked with a preoccupied, almost furtive, manner. For twenty minutes the boys trailed him, while he wandered about apparently looking for something. At first they adopted extreme caution, but soon, reassured by the fact that the man seemed completely oblivious of their presence, they were sauntering after him with complete confidence.

At length he sat down on a low wall and began undoing the fastenings of his case.

"Surely he can't be going to start transmitting now," whispered Peter.

John was watching the articles which were being removed from the case; they had a regrettably familiar appearance.

"I think he's going to paint a picture," he said.

It was too true. The man was setting up a folding easel and arranging his painting materials conveniently on the wall.

After this experience they became used to disappointment. They watched a man for some time who was pacing up and down in an agitated manner, looking at his watch. However, when a young woman arrived, his agitation vanished and he moved off by her side with a slightly inane expression on his face.

"Come on," said John disgustedly. "Let's have a bathe."

Peter muttered something about a " cover plan ", but in their hearts both boys knew that they were bathing because they enjoyed it and were getting tired of chasing false scents.

"Bother," said Peter, while they were dressing again. He picked up a button which had fallen off the old blazer he was wearing.

"What are you worrying about? You've still got two perfectly good buttons." John was feeling a lot better after his bathe.

Peter did not reply immediately. He stood gazing at the button in his hand. "I've got an idea," he said at length. " It was the button which reminded me. You remember that Miss Stiggins told us that she would sew any buttons on for us."

" You're not going to worry about having a button off," John broke in scornfully.

" No, but it'll be an excuse for going to see her. You know how interested she always is in everyone else's business? We might work the conversation round that way and then ask her is she's seen anyone odd. She's bound to know if there was anyone."

" Jolly good idea, Pete." John was full of enthusiasm. " But what excuse can we give for wanting to know about suspicious characters?"

" I can't imagine."

Both boys stood lost in thought.

" Let's get something to eat," said John at length. " We might think of something while we're eating."

It was about half-way through his second sausage roll that inspiration came to John.

" You know how newspapers have a man who goes round seaside places and the first person who says ' Mr. Snobby Snooks ', or something of that sort, gets a guinea."

" It sounds a bit odd. Have you ever seen Mr. Snobby Snooks?" Peter asked.

" No," John admitted. " But I'm sure I've read about it. Anyhow, what I suggest is that we say some boy's paper is running a competition for young detectives and you have to spot the suspicious character."

" Do you think that she'll swallow that?"

" I should think so. Anyhow, let's try. Come on."

Miss Stiggins took a long time to answer their knock and, when she did arrive, seemed rather surprised to see them. But when they explained about the button, she welcomed them in.

" Come in, dear boys. Of course I'll sew it on for you." And she led them into the sitting-room of the cottage.

It was a low, darkish room with oak beams and small windows. Over the fireplace was a collection of horse brasses; round the walls and on various pieces of furniture was a most miscellaneous assortment of china; in one corner was a spinning-wheel. The furniture was mostly old and rather battered, so that a new sewing-machine in one corner looked somewhat out of place.

" Sit down, dear boys, and give me your coat. I'll see what I can do."

Peter sat down. John remained standing, wondering furiously how he could introduce the subject of the competition.

" Shall I get the sewing-machine?" he asked by way of conversation making, and moved towards the machine.

" Of course not," said Miss Stiggins, speaking quite sharply. " You silly boy, surely you know that you don't want a machine for sewing on buttons."

" I'm sorry," John mumbled, and sat in a chair which appeared to have been specially designed to present the maximum number of sharp edges to anyone rash enough to sit in it.

" And what are you dear boys doing now you are on your own?" Miss Stiggins asked.

The opening was too good to miss and John took it. " We are going in for a competition," he said, and explained how they were looking for suspicious characters.

" And you two are young detectives? You do have fun nowadays. I would never have thought of doing anything like that when I was a girl." Miss Stiggins gave a little giggle.

" We were wondering if you could help us," Peter put in. " We thought that you might have seen someone odd."

" Oh dear me, I don't think that I can. Let me see." Miss Stiggins's sewing got slower and slower while she thought, until at times the hand holding her needle remained poised motionless in the air. " I did see a man with a black beard in Barton yesterday," she said at length. " He seemed to be a foreigner. Would he be any good?"

The boys exchanged glances.

" I hope so," said John. " Thank you so much for helping us."

Miss Stiggins handed Peter his coat, now complete with buttons. " Well, I do hope that I may have been useful. Do let me know if you win the competition."

It seemed as if the visit to Miss Stiggins had changed the boys' luck. They had barely got back to Barton when they saw a man, with a great black beard which came down to his collar, emerge from a boarding-house. There was no need for any comment. Both boys knew that this was their man.

He was not tall but very broad. His arms were disproportionately long, and this, combined with a somewhat shambling way of walking, gave him an ape-like appearance.

He was dressed in a shabby dark suit, the pockets of which were so full that it made his outline even broader and more grotesque than before. A pair of glasses with tinted lenses completed his appearance.

As he stepped into the street, he stretched himself and yawned as if he had just awoken from sleep. He looked up at the clear sky, gave a grunt of pleasure, looked up and down the street, and then set off towards the sea. The boys followed.

When he reached a bus stop he paused, took out his watch and began pacing up and down. The boys sat down on a near-by seat.

" It shouldn't be difficult to trace him," Peter remarked. " Anyone could spot him a mile off."

" Yes," said John. " I wonder what he'd look like without his beard. It might be false."

" I suppose that it might," Peter replied thoughtfully.

These speculations were interrupted by the arrival of the bus. Among the passengers was a youngish man wearing a mackintosh jacket, old grey flannel trousers and strong boots; he carried a haversack on his back. The bearded man greeted him warmly.

The boys were too far away to hear what was said, but one thing they could distinguish clearly. The youngish man was English, but the bearded man spoke with a heavy guttural accent.

The two men walked off together and entered a teashop called Peg's Pantry. The boys regarded the place with some distrust. It did not look the sort of place which would provide the tea which they were needing, but they followed the men inside.

The inside of Peg's Pantry bore a strong resemblance to Ivy Cottage. It was low, with beams and plaster. As an added attraction the waitresses wore eighteenth-century dress with mob caps, in which they looked slightly uncomfortable. John felt that Miss Stiggins would have loved the place.

It had one great advantage for their purpose. The room was very irregular in shape and, when the two men had sat down, the boys were able to obtain a table which was out of sight, but sufficiently near to give them a chance of overhearing the conversation.

They ordered two teas from a rather disdainful waitress and tried to catch as much as possible of what was being said at the next table.

For the moment the two men were merely talking about the bus journey and other unimportant matters. The bearded man, they found, spoke excellent English despite his foreign accent.

The teas, when they arrived, confirmed their worst fears. They were definitely of the dainty variety with thin slices of bread and butter and neat little cakes.

It was about this time that they discovered a disadvantage in their position. The door to the kitchen was just opposite and, whenever it was open, the clatter of crockery drowned any conversation from the next table. As the place filled up, the door was opening constantly.

" I wish that they'd spend a little more on food and a bit less on fancy dress for the waitresses," grumbled Peter as he swallowed one of the dainty pieces of bread and butter in a single mouthful. John did not reply; he had just overheard a remark from the next table.

" Then you think that to-night will be suitable," the younger man was saying.

" I do. Zat is why I telephoned you."

" Where is the apparatus?"

" I haf it in my lodgings. I zink . . ." The deep rumbling voice was drowned by the clatter as a waitress emerged from the kitchen.

For some time they could only hear broken snatches of conversation which did not make any sense. The teashop was almost full now and the waitresses were hurrying in and out of the kitchen, slightly hindered by their cumbersome clothing.

" What about paying our bill now?" said Peter. " Then we can nip out quickly. We don't want them to see us."

" Good idea," replied John.

They had just paid when the deep voice once more became audible.

" Let us depart now. Ve vill go to my lodging and I vill explain exactly how my plan vorks."

" Right, and if we set out at six that should give us plenty of time."

" Vaitress." The voice rose to a bellow, which made one waitress jump so much that she nearly dropped a teapot. " I vant my bill."

" Quick," said John. " Let's get out. If we're

watching his lodging by quarter past six," he added when they were outside, " that should be plenty of time. What shall we do till then?"

" Do?" retorted Peter. " Let's get some tea. I'm starving."

BY a quarter to six the boys were concealed in an archway, from which they could watch the door of the boarding-house some fifty yards away. They had discovered by an earlier reconnaissance that there was no back entrance to the boarding-house.

Behind them, farther under the archway, were their bicycles. They had decided that it would be better if they separated while trailing Blackbeard. Peter, who was the smaller of the two, would keep him in sight on foot; John, riding his own bicycle and pushing Peter's, would keep Peter in sight. If Peter wanted John to join him, he would give a signal by raising one arm over his head.

Punctually at six the two men emerged from the boarding-house. Blackbeard was carrying a black case slung from his shoulder by a broad leather strap; clearly this must be the " apparatus ". The other man was carrying a large haversack containing, amongst other things, what looked like a light tent.

The two men walked towards the sea and then turned towards the stretch of moorland which lay between Barton and the mouth of the River Girdle. When they were about a hundred yards away Peter slipped out of the archway and began walking after them. As Peter turned the corner John followed with the bicycles.

At first all went well. There were plenty of people about near the beach and Peter had no difficulty in keeping the men in sight without making himself conspicuous. John dropped back a bit so that he was a couple of hundred yards behind.

As the men got farther from the village the people and houses thinned out. John saw Peter begin to move more cautiously. Eventually he stopped under the cover of the corner of an old concrete pill-box— a relic of the war—and remained there so long that John wondered what had happened. He was just about to leave the bicycles and join Peter when the latter raised his hand above his head.

" Look," said Peter when John had joined him.

John looked round the corner of the pill-box. The road turned slightly inland and ran dead straight for a mile, rising slightly and without a scrap of cover. The two men were about a quarter of a mile away.

" They'll spot us as soon as we leave here," he said.

" I know," Peter replied. " But I've an idea. They've never seen us, have they?"

" No, not well enough to recognize us."

" Well, suppose we bicycle past them and try and shadow them from ahead."

" Jolly good idea, Pete!" cried John enthusiastically. " Come on, let's get cracking."

They leapt on their bicycles and set off down the road. When they overtook the men they bent forward over the handlebars, pedalling furiously, in order to hide their faces as much as possible. As far as John could see, the two men only gave them a casual glance.

When they were over the crest of the rise the boys slowed down, and here another difficulty met them: the road divided. Ahead was a small hill. The main road dipped down, passing to the left of this hill. To the right a track ran off. This passed over the right shoulder of the hill, behind which it disappeared. Farther on the track could be seen climbing the ridge of high ground between the sea and the river.

" What do we do now?" asked Peter, looking at John.

John's forehead was wrinkled; he was thinking hard. " I think we must wait here to see which way they go. After all, it would be natural for us to have a rest after a race."

" O.K.," said Peter. After a pause he added: " What about starting ragging about when they come into sight. It might prevent their recognizing us again."

" Come on, then," replied John, gripping Peter's leg. For the heads of the two men had just appeared over the crest of the hill.

As they came nearer it was clear that the " apparatus " was heavy, as Blackbeard was sweating freely despite his ape-like physique. By the time that they were abreast the boys, John was lying on Peter's head while Peter's heels were kicking in the air.

" Ach, the energy of the young," remarked

Blackbeard to his companion as they swung down the main road.

As soon as the men were past both boys sat up. John had had time to think things out.

"We must go along the track and watch from there," he said. "They won't be able to see us from the dip in the road."

"But they'll see us once we're clear of the small hill," Peter objected.

"If we go on our bicycles we ought to be able to make the crest of the ridge before they're round the hill. Let's see. It must be half a mile before they'll be out of the dip. They're not walking fast, so that'll give us about ten minutes. We'll keep going for nine. Come on. There's not much time."

There was no time for further protest by Peter. The boys were soon speeding along the track, bending low over the handlebars to reduce the chance of being seen. After the first few hundred yards the lower slopes of the hill effectively screened them from the road.

They made good progress to the shoulder of the hill, but after this the track began to get rougher. The downhill run was a series of shattering bumps and hairbreadth skimming of boulders.

"I should think that my wheels will be square after this," Peter gasped. "It feels as if they're getting that way already."

John did not reply; he was looking at his watch. By the time that they had reached the bottom and begun to climb up to the ridge, five of their precious minutes had gone.

With the slope against them and the track getting rougher than ever, progress was desperately slow. John kept on looking at his watch.

" Nearly eight minutes gone. We'll never make it," he gasped.

The moor was wilder and more broken. About a hundred yards ahead was a large rock some five feet high by the side of the path.

" Come on," said John. " Let's get behind that."

They dragged the bicycles behind the rock and flung themselves, panting, on the bracken. They were just in time. Within a minute two figures appeared on the road from behind the small hill.

The two men made their way steadily along the road. As they advanced, the boys climbed up towards the top of the ridge in order to keep them in sight. There was little risk of their being seen, as the men were by now half a mile away and the moor offered a fair amount of cover.

At length they reached a position, near the top of the ridge, which commanded a view of almost the whole road. They saw that it led to a lighthouse on the point.

When the men were about a mile from the lighthouse, they turned off the road towards the sea and, after a short distance, disappeared into a hollow in the moor. The boys waited for them to emerge. Five minutes passed and still there was no sign of them.

" We must have seen them if they had gone on," said John, more to himself than to Peter.

" Then they are still in that hollow," Peter grunted. " What is the next move?"

John had been considering this problem for some time and had his answer ready. " One of us must keep them under observation. The other must go back to The Haven and bring Uncle George and Mr. Baxter along."

There was a pause. Both boys wanted to stay, but in his heart Peter knew that he was not as good as John at shadowing the men on the moor.

" I'll go back," he volunteered.

John did not say anything, but Peter knew that he understood.

" I'll meet you here in an hour's time," Peter went on.

" Thanks, Pete. I'll be here."

John watched Peter descend the track to the rock, collect his bicycle and ride off. He then turned to the question of finding out what was happening in the hollow.

Neither man was visible, but, if he made a direct approach, there was always the risk that one of them might emerge and see him. There was also the possibility that they might be watching from some concealment.

He decided to cross the ridge and make his way along the far side, which would bring him within a few hundred yards of the hollow. By then it would be getting dark and he might be able to approach and discover what was going on.

He put his plan into execution immediately. Moving carefully to avoid being silhouetted against the sky, he crossed the ridge. He then moved quickly along the far slope until he was close to a pile of rocks, which he had noted as being the point where the ridge approached nearest to the hollow. Making use of the cover these afforded, he crept cautiously to the crest and looked over.

He found that he could see into the hollow. Although the light was beginning to fade, he could make out a tent and something which looked like a long thin rod rising in front of it.

Although the tent was probably invisible from the road, it was only a short distance from it. It struck John that the men must be very confident, for they did not appear to be keeping much of a look-out. Encouraged by this, he began moving down the slope with the idea of getting more information. After a short distance he paused. The long thin rod was now clearly visible.

" It must be an aerial," he said to himself. " It couldn't be anything else."

If it was an aerial, then these must be the men they were looking for, so it would be absurd to risk going any nearer. He might be discovered and the men would escape before Uncle George arrived. Obviously his best plan was to go back.

But John did not start back at once. The thought had struck him that he might really be turning back because he was frightened to go on and not because it was the best plan.

" Anyhow, it would be jolly silly to go on just to show that I'm not frightened," he muttered. And with this reflection he made his way back to the top of the ridge.

From his look-out he resumed his watch on the

hollow, occasionally casting an eye down the track for signs of Peter returning with Uncle George and Mr. Baxter.

John wished that he had some field-glasses. It was getting pretty dark by now and he could not see much in the hollow. Fortunately the men appeared to have some sort of light in the tent. From time to time this disappeared as if they were moving about between him and the light, but this was the only indication of their presence.

He thought of having a closer look, but nearly an hour had passed since Peter had left and it was time he started back for the rendezvous.

It took John longer than he expected to make his way across the moor in the dark and he was five minutes late reaching the rendezvous. However, the others had not arrived. After another twenty minutes' waiting John began to get anxious. Perhaps Peter had missed them. He wondered what he ought to do.

Obviously it would be no use trying to tackle the men himself. He might go to the police. But would they believe him? He doubted it. Anyhow, he was sure that Uncle George did not want a lot of publicity. He decided that the only possible thing would be to keep a close watch on the men and see what they did. He would give the others three-quarters of an hour's grace and then set out.

There were still another five minutes to go when he saw something approaching up the track. When it got nearer he could make out three figures and heard Peter call " John " softly. John gave a sigh of relief.

"Here," he answered, and stood up.

"I'm sorry we're late," said Peter, "but it took longer than I'd expected. I'd quite forgotten that we wouldn't be able to use our bikes on the track in the dark."

John explained what he'd seen in the hollow. If he had expected that Uncle George would be excited, he was disappointed. Uncle George spoke in his normal calm voice.

"Good work. It looks as if you've had a lucky break. Now lead us to this place where we can see down into the hollow."

It was fortunate that John had done the journey twice already. Even though the moon was beginning to rise and it was getting rather lighter, all John's powers were needed to find the sheep tracks leading to the pile of rocks. Once there, Uncle George produced a pair of powerful night-glasses and studied the hollow. The light in the tent was clearly visible.

"Yes, I can make out the aerial," grunted Uncle George after a careful survey. "It's odd they haven't shaded that light, though. Now for our plan of action."

He looked round the little group. Both boys felt keyed up with a funny tingling sensation under their scalps. It was just like walking out to the wicket in your first important match, thought John.

"If they make a break for it," said Uncle George, "they'll probably go for the road. Baxter, you go between the tent and the road; John, take the right; Peter, the left; I'll go in front. And remember, you boys, if they do make a break for it, take 'em low with a proper rugger tackle. That'll bring any man down. Come on."

They set off in single file down the hill. Neither Blackbeard nor his companion could be seen; both appeared to be inside the tent. When they crossed the road they paused, and Uncle George and Mr. Baxter slipped off their haversacks, leaving them by the side of the road. Thus lightened for action, they spread out and moved to their positions round the tent.

The entrance of the tent was to seaward and, as both men were still inside, there was a good chance of surprising them, if the approach was silent.

As the moon rose it became easier to see. The four moved slowly and silently forward until they formed a semicircle round the tent. Uncle George took a quick look at the others to make sure that they were in position, drew something from his pocket and stepped swiftly in front of the opening of the tent.

For several seconds there was complete silence. John could see Uncle George looking into the tent. He did not know quite what he had expected— shouts, sudden movements, perhaps shots. But when the silence was broken, the sound that came out of the tent was the last that he had expected to hear— a great bellow of bass laughter.

"What can have gone wrong?" thought John. "There is certainly a wireless set there."

His thoughts were interrupted by Blackbeard's

voice. " But, George, if you vant to come and vatch, vy do you appear so dramatically?"

Uncle George was signalling to them to join him. Whatever may have been going on in his mind, he neither looked nor sounded disconcerted.

" This is my old friend Professor Ksk, the famous ornithologist," he said.

" And this," said the Professor, " is Mr. Brown, the secretary of the local bird-watching society, who is helping me with my experiment. And these two young men," looking at John and Peter, " are they ornithologists too?"

" They have given me a lot of help in my work," replied Uncle George, smiling. " The Professor has a theory that migrating birds can detect wireless waves," he went on. " So he has been transmitting on his wireless set to see if he can observe any effect on the birds."

" Ve hope to see some results to-morrow morning. Can you join us?" said the Professor.

" Thank you, no. We mustn't interrupt your work. I just looked in as I thought it must be you. Good-bye." Uncle George led the party back to the road.

It was about time. The boys could not have concealed their surprise and disappointment much longer. The whole plan had collapsed like a house of cards.

" I'm awfully sorry making a silly mistake like that," said John in a gloomy voice.

Uncle George laughed. " It was a bit of a smack in the face, wasn't it? But don't take it too much to heart. You have to get used to disappointment in this game. You often follow several false trails before you hit the right one."

" Did they see your pistol?" asked Peter.

" I don't think so. I slipped it back into my pocket pretty quick. When the Professor is thinking about birds, I doubt if he'd have noticed if I'd produced a blunderbuss."

Mr. Baxter had been collecting the haversacks during this conversation. " What you youngsters want is some of this," he said.

This was a thermos of hot, sweet cocoa. It gave the boys a warm glow inside.

" Thanks awfully," said Peter. " I feel better already."

" When you've been at sea for twenty years you don't start on a trip like this without taking a few precautions." And Mr. Baxter began filling his beloved pipe.

" Well, let's get on back home," said Uncle George as they set off along the road.

" Gosh!" John burst out suddenly. " I've just remembered. My bike's still under the rock up the track."

" H'm," said Uncle George. " Obviously not one of our more successful evenings."

BREAKFAST at The Haven next day was not a cheerful meal. Uncle George was silent and preoccupied. The boys, in addition to the disappointment of the previous night's fiasco, were not much cheered by the thought that they were due back at school in a couple of days.

Both John and Peter enjoyed school, but the thought of French irregular verbs acquired an added distaste when compared with the excitement of chasing foreign miscreants.

Only Mr. Baxter was quite unperturbed. After breakfast he lit his pipe and went on board the *Fulmar* to do some repairs to her rigging.

Peter was the first to break a long silence. " Do you think that all the wireless signals were made by the Professor?" he asked.

" I'm not sure. I'm expecting a telephone call some time this morning after the wireless experts have gone into it," said Uncle George. " You see, it was largely a hunch of mine that they would try to smuggle the Iconium out from round here. The hunch may have been wrong. There's another area farther south which is just as suitable. Perhaps we ought to try there. I wonder——" He relapsed into

4   49   (G 781)

silence, drumming on the table with his finger-tips.

At last Peter could bear it no longer. " Can we come and help?" he burst out.

Uncle George looked up. It was obvious that his thoughts had been far away. " Come and help?" he repeated slowly. " I'm afraid not. You see, it may be days or weeks before we get on to anything. You're due back at school in two days, aren't you?"

" Yes," said Peter.

There was another pause and Uncle George resumed his drumming on the table.

" You never told us if you found any coves yesterday, where a boat could get in without being seen," said John.

" You're still sticking to that open Bible clue, aren't you?" John grinned. " Well, as a matter of fact," Uncle George continued, " we did find a very suitable little cove on the north bank of the river near the mouth. It is just the far side of that ridge where you hid last night. The trouble is that there are plenty of suitable places on this coast."

" What is it called?" John asked.

" Sandy Cove, according to the chart. You might like to have a look at it. It's a very pretty spot with no houses near. It can only be two or three miles from here by land."

Both boys made polite noises, but neither was able to work up very much enthusiasm over Sandy Cove. Altogether it was a pretty grim morning.

It was twelve when Uncle George's telephone call came through. It took a long time and, when he came back, he did not look much more cheerful.

"Like most experts, he put in so many possibilities that it's very hard to know exactly what he thinks," Uncle George said in answer to the unspoken inquiry on the boys' faces. "There may have been some other signals. That's about as far as he'll commit himself."

Owing to the delay caused by the telephone call, the ebb tide was almost done. There was little wind, and Uncle George decided to have lunch and then set off, in the hope that the wind would get up during the meal. It was a vain hope. By the end of lunch there was a flat calm.

"Well," said Uncle George philosophically, "there's no helping it. We'll have to go out on the engine. It's going to be a slow business with the tide against us the whole way."

"Looks like wind, though," said Mr. Baxter, gazing up into the sky. "Maybe we'll get some later."

Twenty minutes later the boys stood on the hard, watching the *Fulmar* moving slowly down river.

"I wanted to have a last sail this afternoon," said John, "but there isn't even enough wind to give the dinghy steerage way."

"What about having a look at Sandy Cove as there's nothing better to do?"

"I suppose that we might as well. Let's take some food with us. We can clear up the house this evening. We'd better ring up for a taxi for to-morrow."

Collecting food took some time, for John's heart was not really in the job. He had barely finished

51

stowing the haversack when Peter, who had been telephoning for the taxi, reappeared.

"Telephone's bust," he announced. "I can't get a cheep out of it."

"This would happen," said John. "It's that sort of a day. I suppose we can telephone from Ivy Cottage. I saw that there were telephone wires there. I suppose that means having a cosy chat with Miss Stiggins and answering a lot of silly questions."

John's suppositions were cut short by Peter. "You needn't worry. Look who's coming."

John joined Peter at the window. Miss Stiggins herself was approaching on her bicycle.

"Quick, let's hide and pretend we're not at home," said Peter.

"Too late. She's seen us." For Miss Stiggins had just given a wave of such resolute cheeriness that it nearly caused her to fall off her bicycle.

"Dear boys," she said when they opened the door, "I thought that I might have missed you, when I saw the boat going away."

"No; we're going back to school to-morrow," answered Peter.

"I hoped to sell you all some tickets for a raffle. Are you two dear boys all alone?"

"Yes. My uncle and his friend have gone off again," John replied. "They just came in to see us."

"And you dear boys were left behind because you have to go back to school. What a pity! What a pity! Well, perhaps you would like to take a ticket. They're only sixpence and you can win all

sorts of prizes. Let me see if I can find the list."
And Miss Stiggins began fumbling in her bag.

The boys looked at one another. Both thought
that to get rid of Miss Stiggins for sixpence was
cheap at the price. When they turned back towards
Miss Stiggins, she had stopped fumbling in her bag,
but she had not produced a list of prizes. They found
themselves looking down the barrel of an automatic
pistol.

Miss Stiggins's eyes still gleamed as benevolently
as ever behind her glasses, but the hand that held the
pistol was as steady as a rock. The click as she flicked
off the safety catch had the air of professional com-
petence.

" Perhaps you would put your hands above your
heads and turn and face the wall."

The boys remained motionless. The surprise had
left them incapable of movement and they stood
goggling at Miss Stiggins. There was a muffled
report; a bullet buried itself in the wall behind
John's head. John felt as if the tip of his left ear had
been burnt with a hot iron. Like a flash both pairs
of hands shot into the air and the boys spun round
to face the wall.

" Dear boys," Miss Stiggins's voice posivitely
cooed, " you will have to learn to obey orders
more quickly in future. If I have to shoot again it
will be much more painful."

She broke off and called out something in a foreign
language. The boys heard the door open and someone came in.

" All right, you can turn round now and put

your hands down. Vassili won't stand any nonsense, I warn you."

The boys turned and had their first sight of the newcomer. His appearance did little to reassure them.

He had a bullet head, with close-cropped hair and flat Mongolian features. His teeth were broken and uneven, and his dull eyes gave an occasional flicker of an almost animal ferocity. His hands were broad and immensely powerful, with thick stubby fingers, one of which had the top joint missing. It was obvious that he was as hard as nails, and John realized that, apart from Miss Stiggins's pistol, any idea of making a dash for it would be hopeless.

"You haven't seen Vassili before, my two young detectives," said Miss Stiggins in a mocking voice. "It was very thoughtful of you, though, to ask my advice yesterday. While you were all having your little games with Professor Ksk, Vassili was able to prepare a little surprise for your uncle." Miss Stiggins gave one of her little giggles. "I hope that you weren't very fond of your uncle, because I'm afraid that you won't see him again. His yacht will be destroyed by a mysterious explosion. They'll probably have an inquest and decide that the engine must have exploded. Everybody will say that it was very sad. Dear boys!" Miss Stiggins positively beamed with benevolence.

By this time John had recovered from his stunned surprise. His ear was still hurting and he could feel occasional drops of blood coursing down his neck. But the pain in his ear was the least of his worries.

Uncle George was in deadly danger, partly through his fault, and he could do nothing to save him. Also it looked as if Miss Stiggins and her associates were going to have a clear run for getting the Iconium out of the country. He racked his brains for some solution, but the more he considered the situation, the more hopeless it seemed.

Miss Stiggins had been talking with Vassili in a foreign language, and John's thoughts were interrupted by another of her little giggles.

"You boys are a great nuisance," she said. "I thought that you'd be on board the yacht and disappear neatly with the others. Vassili wants to cut your throats, but bodies are so difficult to get rid of in this country and, if they were found, it might be most awkward for me."

She paused while she slipped the pistol back into her bag. "I suppose that Vassili could drown you and then upset the boat, as if it had been an accident. But then someone might see him. Really you are the most provoking boys."

John looked at Peter and was glad to see an expression of relief on his face. John had no great relish for either drowning of having his throat cut. The fact that Miss Stiggins had rejected both alternatives gave him some slight comfort, and Peter apparently felt the same.

Miss Stiggins had been indulging in another lengthy discussion with Vassili. She appeared to be asking a lot of questions to which Vassili replied mostly with a series of short grunts. Finally Miss Stiggins turned back to the boys, beaming. The touch of peevishness which had been noticeable just previously had gone. Her voice was unctuous, making John feel as if something sticky was being poured over him.

"Dear boys, I have such a treat for you. We have decided that Vassili shall take you with him. He thinks that with a little ' training ' you might become quite nice boys. He promises that he will look after your ' training ' himself. Won't that be fun for you? I'm afraid that first we'll have to lock you up for a bit, though."

Miss Stiggins led the way out of the room. She seemed to be quite familiar with the geography of the house. Vassili seized the boys by the arm and pulled them after her, ignoring their struggles. He might have been holding a couple of kittens. John felt as if he had been gripped by a machine.

"All right," said Peter angrily. "You needn't hold my arm so tight."

Vassili paid not the slightest attention.

"I'm afraid that Vassili does not understand much English," Miss Stiggins remarked. "In fact the only word he knows is Iconium, and that isn't really English, is it? But it did enable him to get my message in Barton Church, that the coast was clear, except, of course, for you dear boys."

Miss Stiggins led them to the larder and opened the door. "This should do very nicely," she said.

It was only too true. The larder might have been made for the purpose. It was a small room with a stone floor. Round three walls ran a broad stone shelf supported by stout iron supports. There was only one window, small and high up, with heavy wooden shutters. The wooden door was massive with an old-fashioned lock to match.

Miss Stiggins closed and barred the shutters. "Just in case you thought of shouting for help," she added, beaming.

It seemed to John that this was a fairly futile precaution as they could easily open the shutters again once they were alone. But Miss Stiggins had not finished. She said something to Vassili, who produced two pairs of handcuffs out of his pocket.

Miss Stiggins had taken her pistol from her bag again. While she covered Peter, Vassili seized John and put the handcuffs on him so that one of the iron supports was between his arms. He then secured Peter in a similar manner to one of the supports on the opposite wall.

There was no question of opening the shutters now. The boys could only sit or squat on the floor. The support between their arms restricted their movements to a couple of feet at the most.

"Dear boys, you don't look very comfortable," said Miss Stiggins.

Vassili gave a grunt, emptied the boys' pockets and left them, slamming the door. The boys heard the lock grind into place and the key withdrawn. The footsteps died away and there was silence.

The boys screwed themselves round so that they could see one another.

"Well," said Peter cheerfully, "I don't think that we can possibly be on a false trail this time."

THE boys looked round their prison. With its
solid walls, door and shutters, it looked remarkably secure.

"Do you think that we could make anyone hear
if we shouted!" Peter asked.

"I doubt it. Very few people come round here,
but we can try. It's our only hope. Let's wait five
minutes till they are well away and then try. They
might hear us if we shouted now."

It was a very long five minutes. John still had his
wrist-watch and he kept on looking at it to be quite
sure that it had not stopped, so slowly did time go.

"Now," said John at last.

Both boys took a deep breath and then started.
"Help! Help!" The shouts echoed from the bare
walls and floor. Inside the room the noise was
terrific. It sounded like a football match with the
Home Side about to score.

When they were both out of breath they stopped.
The house was completely silent, except for a slight
scuffling noise as if a mouse was retiring to a quieter
spot.

"Let's try again," said John.

Once more they used their lungs to their full

capacity until they were out of breath. Once more they listened. This time they thought that they could hear someone. In a minute they were certain. Someone was coming in at the front door.

"We're in here. Help!" they shouted.

The footsteps approached the door. They heard the key inserted; the lock groaned as it moved; the door swung open and Vassili entered.

Without a word he gave both boys a blow on the side of the head, which made them see stars and feel slightly sick. He then relocked the door and departed.

"Gosh!" said John, cooling his throbbing head against the cool stone shelf. "That wasn't very funny."

"No," agreed Peter. "I don't think that we're going to like Vassili's 'training' a bit. I wish I had some idea how we could get out."

John did not reply; he was working his wrists in his handcuffs.

"Pete," he said, "I think I can see a chance. You remember that chap who called himself an 'escapist' or something like that."

"The one in the circus whom we got to know?"

"Yes, that one. He showed me a trick you can do if someone is putting handcuffs on you. You brace your muscles in a certain way, so that your wrists swell. Then you relax and the handcuffs are loose."

"Do you mean that you can slip yours off?"

"I don't know. I tried bracing my muscles but it didn't seem to work. I suppose it must have been because we were struggling with that gorilla Vassili."

" I reckon that you're being jolly rude to gorillas,"
said Peter, who found it difficult to be downhearted
for very long.

" Anyhow, they feel much looser now. I'm going
to try and slip my hands out."

" Good-oh."

For the next few minutes the room was filled with
the sounds of heavy breathing, grunts and exclam-
ations of pain from John, against a background of
metallic noises as the chain of the handcuffs sawed
to and fro around the support as he struggled.

" Ouch!" he exclaimed at last, sucking a thumb
from which most of the skin had been scraped. An
empty handcuff dangled from his left wrist: his right
hand was free.

Peter had also been making unavailing attempts
to free himself, but the handcuffs were tight on
his wrists and he could not move them at all.

John bent down to examine them and see if there
was any way of undoing them. It was hopeless.
A special key was required to unlock them and the
chain was far too strong to be broken without proper
tools.

" John, you go on. Escape and warn the others.
I'll be all right."

" Thanks, Pete. You mayn't be remarkable for
your beauty, but you do look better in one piece.
If Vassili finds you here and me gone, he'd——"
John paused. It did not do to dwell on the prospect.
" No, we stick together," he finished up.

The problem was how to release Peter. The iron
support was an inch thick. There was no hope of

breaking that. Both boys pulled it with all their strength. It shook very slightly. Again they tried, with the same result.

They looked at the bottom end. It was cemented into the floor. The top end was not cemented and John could move it a little, but it was embedded in the stone shelf. There was no hope of pulling it out.

John was examining the shelf from above and Peter, being still handcuffed, perforce from below.

Suddenly Peter said: "There are two cracks in the bottom of the stone. Do you think they go right through? We might be able to lift a bit of the shelf off the top of the support."

John bent down and examined the cracks. He traced the rough line of them round the edge of the shelf with his finger and found that they could continue across the top, though the crack was so small that he had not been able to see it.

"Let's try," he said.

Both boys put their shoulders under the shelf and heaved. A great slab of stone lifted a bit. It was immensely heavy and was not made any easier to lift by having one end embedded in the wall.

"Once more," said John. "Ready now. Heave ho!"

The boys struggled with all their strength. Slowly the great slab lifted until it was just clear of the support, where it seemed to stick. Then Peter's foot slipped and the slab fell back into place with a thud and clouds of dust.

"Rot it!" said Peter. "I thought we had got it clear."

He looked at John and stopped. John's forehead was wrinkled in thought. Peter knew that it was a waste of time talking to John when he was looking like that.

"Obviously we aren't strong enough to get the slab right off," said John at length. "I suppose the wall must have been holding it. If we can hold it just clear of the top of the support, could you slip your chain through the gap?"

"I'll try. I've got my breath back now and I'm ready for another shot."

Once more with immense effort they lifted the slab. When the gap appeared big enough, Peter tried to flick his chain through. In doing so he had to relax his efforts to lift the stone. It fell back and caught the chain between it and the top of the support. Peter was now pinioned close to the slab and had difficulty in getting his shoulder under it.

There was little time to get their breath, for Peter was in a cramped, uncomfortable position. Once more they made a great effort. Once more, just as the slab was coming clear, Peter's foot slipped. But this time he fell backwards and in falling tore the chain clear.

Peter lay on his back on the floor, dirty, sore and still handcuffed, but free to move about. "Gosh!" he said. "That's a bit better."

John climbed on to the shelf, opened the shutters and peered out.

"Shall we try shouting again, now that we've got the shutters open?" Peter asked.

"I don't think it's worth it, do you? If Vassili is

still about, he'll hear us and find we're free. I can't see anyone from here anyway."

" Then what's the next move? Can we get through the window?"

" I don't think so. The bars seem to be cemented into the stone. I wish we had our knives. We might have chipped it away."

With some difficulty Peter climbed up beside John; he found it awkward moving about with his hands shackled together. They put their full combined weight on the bars but they did not budge even a fraction of an inch. There was no crack in the stonework to offer a hope for the technique they had used on the shelf.

" Let's have a look at the door," said John.

The door was immensely strong. The old master mariner had built his house to last and the doors were solid affairs made of oak. After a few attempts the boys gave up any idea of breaking down the door as hopeless. The massive lock was on their side of the door but it was as immovable as the door itself.

It looked as if the boys had freed themselves from the supports, only to be trapped in the larder. Also time was running short, not only for themselves but also for warning Uncle George. The only hope of warning the *Fulmar* was to catch her before she left the river, and, even with the tide against her, it could not be very long before she had negotiated the great bend round the Pottles and would be heading for the open sea. Neither boy said anything but their thoughts were not cheerful.

John examined the lock carefully. It was secured by four large screws.

"If only we had got our knives we might have tried unscrewing them. As it is——" He became silent and then went on: "Look, Pete, I think we must take the risk and start shouting. Even if Vassili does hear and find us free, we're not much worse off. What do you think?"

But Peter, instead of answering, slapped his hand against his leg and said: "Gosh, I've got an idea! My belt has got a buckle. Could we use that as a screwdriver?" He began struggling to undo his belt.

The belt had a buckle, a strong steel one. With fingers trembling with excitement John tried it in the slot of one of the screws. With a little manœuvring it fitted. John applied pressure and very slowly the screw began to turn.

Removing the screws was a maddeningly slow process, for if John used too much force the edge of the buckle bent. Nevertheless he managed to remove the two outer screws. By this time the edge of the buckle looked like a saw and, when John attempted to start one of the inner screws, bits began to break off the buckle.

"Let's try and pull the lock off the door," said John.

By scrabbling with their fingers they managed to prise the outer end of the lock slightly away from the door. This gave them just enough room to slip the chain of Peter's handcuffs underneath the lock. They both hove away on the chain with all their might. There was a splintering crash. The lock broke away and the door swung slowly open.

Instinctively both boys stood absolutely rigid, listening. Was Vassili watching? Had their escape been overheard? Were they really free at last? For a full half minute they stood. The silence was complete. Then John rushed to the telephone.

"I'll get the police," he said. "They must believe us now."

Barton telephone exchange had not yet reached the stage of being automatic and calls often took some time before they were answered. Peter saw John rattle the calling switch, wait a few seconds and then rattle it again.

"There's not a sound, Pete," he said.

"Can I try?" Peter took the receiver, bending his head down as he was unable to lift it to his ear. "It's just like it was when I tried to ring for a taxi."

"I'd forgotten. They must have cut the line before Miss Stiggins came here. It runs just past Ivy Cottage. That woman's no fool whatever she may look like."

"How can we get a message through? Do you think that it would be worth while trying to rush past on our bikes?"

"Can you ride a bike with your handcuffs on?"

"Sounds like a comic song," said Peter, bursting into a roar of laughter. "I think so, if I keep my hands close to the centre of the handlebars, but it'll be a bit awkward for a sprint."

The boys slipped out of the back door, the side of the house away from Ivy Cottage, and studied the road from the shelter of some bushes in the garden. They had seen it often enough before, but never considered it in the light of an escape route. The road ran within a few yards of Ivy Cottage and was absolutely bare of cover once it left the shelter of their garden. On the side of the road away from Ivy Cottage there were only a few yards between the road and the river.

If they could get close to Ivy Cottage without being spotted, they might just slip past but it would be a desperate gamble. Then John saw something else. Miss Stiggins was in the garden, obviously watching the road.

" It's no go," he said. " The road's off." But at that moment something else struck him. The smoke from Ivy Cottage was blowing away to the southward. In the excitement of their escape neither of them had noticed that the wind had got up as Mr. Baxter had prophesied. It was blowing a fresh breeze from the northward.

" The dinghy!" cried Peter. " We'll get out by water."

" Yes, but which way?" replied John more cautiously.

" Past Ivy Cottage, of course. There are houses up that way. There's nothing if we go down by the Pottles."

" But, Pete, will we make it? We'll be beating dead against the wind. They'll see us coming. There's an old rowing boat there, I know. I've seen it. Vassili mayn't be much use on a boat, but in a narrow river like this there would be plenty of

66

time to stop us. And there are no houses until you are round the next bend."

" And if we go downstream we'll never catch the *Fulmar*."

" I know. That's what is worrying me." John became lost in thought, gazing at the river. Suddenly he gave Peter a dig. " Come back into the house. I believe it might be possible."

Back in the house he hurried into the living-room and seized the battered copy of tide tables which was kept there.

" I thought so," he said, pointing. " To-day's an exceptional spring tide, the highest in the year. We might be able to get through the Pottles and drag the dinghy over the causeway. How much time have we?" He looked at his watch. " Let's see. This wind won't help the *Fulmar*. It'll be dead ahead. We've only got about an hour to catch them. We'll have to be jolly quick if we've got to unrig the dinghy, haul her across the causeway and rig her again. Never mind. Let's get cracking."

" We'll have to be jolly quick rigging her if we're to start at all," said Peter. " They're bound to spot us once we're on board."

They hurried out of the house, ran down the garden without any attempt at concealment, and within a minute were on board the dinghy, casting off the lashings on the gear as fast as the handcuffs would allow.

THE dinghy was not a difficult boat to rig, but Peter was handicapped by his handcuffs and John found that the empty handcuff hanging from his left wrist kept on catching on things. He had considered trying to slip his left wrist out, but the removal of the right one had been sufficiently painful to discourage unnecessary experiments in this direction.

Nevertheless, in a couple of minutes they had made good progress with the rigging, when they were disturbed by the sound of a distant shout. They looked round. Miss Stiggins and Vassili had emerged from Ivy Cottage and were running towards them. The distance was between quarter and half a mile and neither Miss Stiggins nor Vassili was built for speed, but it would be touch and go if they would be able to get away.

" Shall I slip the buoy?" asked Peter.

" No good. Tide's still flooding. It would carry us towards them. We've got to get some sail on her. Never mind about the foresail. Give me a hand with this main halliard and get the mainsail up."

" Let's hope that they haven't got a rifle," said Peter as he came aft to help John.

Apparently they had not got a rifle, for the two continued running. Miss Stiggins's miscellaneous collection of garments streamed behind her: the astonishing hat blew off, but she kept close behind Vassili, who had a lumbering bear-like gait.

Slowly the mainsail crept up the mast. John looked over his shoulder. The couple were now a bare hundred yards from the hard. The mainsail was not hoisted as John would have wished, but this was no time for niceties of seamanship.

" Let her go, Pete," he shouted. " We'll have to go like this."

Peter slipped the painter from the buoy. John seized the tiller and hauled on the mainsheet. The sail stopped flapping and filled in the breeze. The boat began slipping through the water, gathering way as she went.

John was fully occupied sailing the boat, but Peter was able to look back. Vassili and Miss Stiggins had arrived on the hard, now some fifty yards astern. Miss Stiggins raised her left elbow till it was level with her face, steadied her pistol on the crook of her elbow and fired.

" Look out!" shouted Peter, ducking.

John followed suit, and at the same moment thrust the tiller hard over so that the boat swerved violently. The bullet struck the stern of the boat within a few inches of John's back, knocking off a shower of splinters. They heard the bullet ricochet off, humming like a bumble bee.

" Gosh!" said Peter. " Jolly good shooting with a pistol at sixty yards."

"Much too good for my taste," replied John.

By this time they were out of range, though not earshot. The remarks on the hard were in a foreign language but, judging by their tone, the atmosphere was not very amicable.

"I don't know what lingo that is," said Peter cheerfully, "but it sounds a good one for letting your friends know exactly what you feel about them."

The boat was sailing, but she was in a state which could scarcely be called shipshape. The mainsail was not properly hoisted; the foresail was not even rigged for hoisting; sail covers, tackles and lashings littered the bottom of the boat. It was clear that Peter could not manage to clear up the mess.

"You take her for a bit," said John. "I'll square things up. We're going to have to sail her all out if we're to catch them."

With Peter at the tiller, John busied himself about the boat and, by the time that they were ready to turn into the creek which led into the Pottles, everything was square and shipshape. It was just as well, for the wind was increasing and was now blowing quite hard in gusts. The elation which John had felt at escaping from Miss Stiggins's clutches was beginning to wear off. In his heart he knew that they would be lucky to catch the *Fulmar* if they had to haul the boat over the causeway; and that, for all he knew, might be impossible.

Before they turned into the creek John took over the tiller. The alteration in course brought the wind before the beam. With the sheets hauled well aft the boat raced through the water.

"D'you think we'll make it?" asked Peter.

"Hope so," said John. "The wind is about as much as she can take like this. If it gets any stronger we'll have to take in a reef."

At one time the Pottles had been farmed. The various islands had been enclosed by sea-walls of earth faced with stone; sheep had grazed there. During a period when agriculture was paying badly, the sea-walls had been allowed to fall into disrepair. The sea had broken through and drowned the islands.

Now they were saltings covered with rank grass, inhabited only by seabirds. On some of the higher bits of land a few stunted trees grew and an occasional ruined shepherd's hut was a relic of the former occupation. Down the centre of the Pottles ran the old causeway, now in poor repair, which was causing John so much anxiety.

As the crow flies the distance across the northern end of the Pottles was a bare couple of miles but, owing to the winding nature of the channels, the distance to be sailed was considerably more.

At high tide the limits of the navigable channels could only be seen from the remains of the sea-walls, since most of the rest of the islands was under water. As the boat rushed down the first stretch of creek, John noticed with some dismay that, owing to the exceptional height of the tide, most of his normal navigation marks were covered. He could only tell the course of the channel from isolated peaks of sea-wall rising from a great sheet of water.

The first bend in the channel presented no difficulties. A patch of higher ground with a ruined cottage on it marked the turning-point. John knew that the water was deep close to the old sea-wall. He altered round to port, easing out the sheets as the wind drew astern.

"Up drop keel," he ordered. "Come aft, Pete. We want to keep the bows up with the wind astern."

Peter was getting used to his handcuffs and was developing a remarkable technique, using both hands for everything.

"O.K.," he said, hauled on the lanyard which hoisted the drop keel, secured it and joined John aft.

The next turn was far more difficult. It was to starboard and would bring the wind right ahead. The next stretch was not long but they would have to tack to and fro in the narrow channel for the whole distance.

John wanted to round the spit of shallow mud at the corner as closely as possible, so as to avoid getting too far to leeward. But if he cut the corner too fine, he would run aground and might capsize.

The trouble was that the spit was covered by the tide. He knew that it ran out some distance beyond the remains of the sea-wall. But how far? He would have to guess the distance. It was a tricky decision and, at the pace at which the boat was travelling, he would have to decide soon.

"Down drop keel," he said as the end of the sea-wall came abeam.

Judging his distance, he brought the boat round

till the wind was abeam, hauling in the sheets as she came up into the wind. Both boys were leaning out over the weather gunwale to trim the boat.

Suddenly Peter gave a yell, " Grass in the water right ahead."

John tugged the tiller towards him and let the sheet run out between his fingers. The boat spun out of the wind, and John saw a great patch of grass and muddy water slip past the starboard side a few feet away.

" That was a bit close," he shouted. Peter grinned in reply.

John let her run fifty yards down wind and then brought her round again. With their eyes skinned for signs of shoal water, the boys hung over the weather side. John glanced to wind'ard. They were past the line of the sea-wall.

" Aft sheets," he cried. " Now we'll see what we can do to windward."

He brought the boat round till she was close hauled on the starboard tack, beating up the next stretch of the channel.

They were now in the loneliest and most desolate part of the Pottles. Ahead they could make out a black line which marked the causeway. This stretched right across their bows and disappeared to the southward behind some low trees and bushes. It did not look a cheerful prospect.

The sky was overcast and the wind was whipping up waves on the grey stretch of water. Curlews disturbed from their nests flew around uttering their mournful cry.

" And to think we came here for a picnic a fort-night ago," remarked Peter.

" Stand by," said John, who was too busy sailing the boat for reminiscence, and a moment later, " Lee oh!"

The boat swung round on to the port tack. During the last leg John had made two unpleasant discoveries. The tide, which should have been slack, was running against them and the boat was carrying too much sail. The latter was the more urgent; he would have to take in a couple of reefs. He dared not risk capsizing the boat as, apart from failing to warn Uncle George, he doubted if Peter could swim in handcuffs.

The boat was fitted with roller reefing. It was merely a matter of lowering the halliards and turning the boom so that the foot of the sail rolled round it like a blind. But this would be quite impossible for Peter. He would have to do this himself.

Also in order to reef, the boat would have to be brought up into the wind to spill the wind out of the sails. During this time she would be drifting to leeward and, on the narrow channel, there was a risk of her drifting ashore. John cursed himself for not reefing earlier when he had more sea-room.

" Pete," he shouted, to make himself heard above the noises in the boat, " I'm going to reef. Will you take her and keep her up into the wind."

He thrust the tiller down till the sails were thrashing about, and nipped forward to the halliards. Peter slipped past him and took the tiller.

With the sail thrashing about, it was a struggle to

74

take the two rolls on the boom. By the time he had secured the boom with the reefing lanyard and re-hoisted the mainsail, the sea-wall was perilously close.

He hurried aft, hauled on the mainsheet till the sail filled and, as soon as the boat had gathered some way, put the tiller down to put her about on the other tack. The boat came up into the wind, hesitated and then stopped. She was aground on the soft mud.

Peter gave a heave which hoisted the drop keel. The boat shook herself, swung round so that the sails filled and began moving through the water. She was free again.

John looked at his watch. With the delay caused by having the tide against them and the reefing, they could only just catch the *Fulmar*, even if they could sail right through the Pottles. There was no margin at all for manhandling the dinghy over the causeway.

" We can't possibly catch the *Fulmar* now, unless she's been delayed," he said. " This foul tide has beaten us."

" I wonder why it should be foul here, when it's slack in the river."

" Dunno. Tides are funny things."

" What can we do?"

" Nothing. Just keep going and hoping *Fulmar's* engine breaks down or something."

They continued beating up the channel, making slow but steady progress. They could see the cause-way more clearly now. Most of it stood two feet above the water and in the gaps the water was breaking, showing that it was very shallow.

" I've got an idea," said Peter.

As this was one of Peter's standard openings, John waited for further details.

" When we were on the picnic," Peter continued, " I went along the causeway exploring. There was a big broken down bit with a stake by it. I've just seen a stake over there, which reminded me of it." He pointed to port. " If someone put a stake there, surely it must mark a channel."

John looked in the direction in which Peter was pointing. There was a gap in the line of trees and bushes, behind which the causeway disappeared. Through the gap a stake was visible. The water near it was not breaking. It looked as if Peter might be right. There might be a gap in the causeway.

John did some very quick thinking. As there was a gap in the line of bushes, there ought to be a creek running towards the stake. John could not remember it from the picnic, but it might have been dry then. They might run aground; they might wreck the boat on the causeway; the creek might be a dead end; all sorts of things might happen; but it was their only hope of catching the *Fulmar*. Even if some or all of the disasters happened, they would not be much worse off. The risk had to be taken. He altered course towards the stake.

" Let's hope you're right," he said.

In the creek the tide against them was stronger, but the wind was now nearly on the beam and the boat could make straight for the gap without tacking.

As the boat tore along, occasional suspicious patches of grass could be seen in the water on either hand, but there was enough water for the boat in the centre of the channel.

They passed the line of the screen of bushes and John could see the stake clearly. It was a great wooden post, bleached and pitted with weather and age. From the top a piece of wood hung by a rusty chain, the remains of an arm to indicate which side the channel lay, so John imagined. Now it hung useless.

" Which side of the stake is the gap?" John asked.

Peter did not answer at once. John glanced at him. There was a look of horror on Peter's face.

" Gosh! I can't remember for certain."

JOHN loved the excitement of sailing. He enjoyed the thrill of the unexpected things which were liable to occur. But this time he felt that the thrills were becoming excessive. No sooner had they avoided one crisis than another cropped up.

They were rushing towards the stake and there was no indication on which side of it the gap in the causeway lay. The tide was flowing through towards then for fifty feet on either side of the stake.

Even as he debated which side to choose, at the back of his mind John realized that this was the explanation of the foul tide which had worried them. The water had piled up against the barrier of the causeway and was now flowing away through the gaps, as well as the channels, towards the sea.

John had been steering straight for the stake, which was now only fifty yards away, in the hope of seeing something to help him to decide which side to go. He could wait no longer. He must choose now.

He decided to pass the weather side of the stake as close as possible. If the channel was the other side, it would be easier to alter to leeward rather then to windward. Soon the stake was abeam, so close that the mast was within a few feet of it. The boat was rushing on unchecked. They were across.

Suddenly the boat gave a great leap. The drop keel shot up, forced from below by some obstruction. The boat heeled over and water poured in over the lee side. She was about to capsize.

Like a flash Peter seized the lanyard of the drop keel and secured it in the hoisted position. John threw his weight as far out to windward as he could manage.

The boat gave two or three sickening lurches accompanied by an awful grinding noise. For a few seconds she hung with her lee gunwale just clear of the water. Then as Peter, firmly clutching hold of the drop keel lanyard to prevent himself going overboard, brought his weight to assist John's, she slowly righted herself. John looked back. The stake was fifty feet astern. They had picked the wrong side but their pace had carried them over the causeway.

The dinghy was over and in a fairly wide creek, but she had a lot of water in her and they did not know what damage she had suffered. John decided that they must bale her out before they sailed any farther. He brought her up into the wind and they began bailing.

After a few minutes' vigorous bailing they had reduced the water to manageable proportions.

"She can't be leaking much at any rate," said John, puffing. "Let's try the drop keel."

Peter released the lanyard and the drop keel slipped down into position.

"Good enough," said John. "Let's push on."

"Suits me," Peter replied. "Bailing in handcuffs is definitely not my idea of fun. What's happened to yours?"

John looked down. The handcuff on his left wrist had disappeared.

"Crippen! I must have pulled it off during the flap crossing the causeway. I never noticed it at the time."

John had never sailed in this part of the Pottles before, but the creek led roughly to the eastward, the direction in which they wanted to go. Some distance ahead there was another line of trees and bushes which John suspected marked the line of the main river.

They were bowling along nicely when Peter shouted, "Look!"

Over the top of the line of bushes the tops of two sails could be seen: the *Fulmar*. While the boys watched, the sails flapped and then filled again as the *Fulmar* went about. Uncle George had taken advantage of the wind and was beating up to the the mouth of the river. Another couple of tacks should be enough to allow her to head for the open sea, John reckoned. In a straightforward race the dinghy had no hope of catching the *Fulmar*. They had to get clear of the creek before the *Fulmar* turned.

"Can they see us?" Peter asked.

"Don't think so. They're too close to those bushes."

John took a grip on the tiller and began driving the dinghy for all she was worth. He considered shaking out a reef but the boat was carrying all the sail she could stand. With the boys hanging over the weather side, soaked with spray, she tore along.

Peter and John were far too busy handling the boat for conversation. As they got close to the line of bushes, they could no longer see the *Fulmar's* sails. They could not tell whether they were going to intercept her or not. At last they passed through the line of the bushes and the estuary of the Girdle was open before them. The *Fulmar* was quarter to half a mile ahead, steering for the open sea.

Now that they were clear of the creek they began to meet the swell coming in from the sea. John could no longer sail the dinghy all out, and the *Fulmar* drew rapidly ahead.

"Uncle George, please, please look astern," Peter kept on repeating to himself.

It was their only hope. For five long minutes nothing happened. John was wondering whether he would have to take in another reef, when he saw the *Fulmar* alter course. She was going about on to the other tack. She had seen them.

"Good old Uncle George! Good old *Fulmar*!" he shouted.

The *Fulmar* was now heading towards them. When she was about a hundred yards away Uncle George brought her into the wind and remained hove to.

"I'll stay in the boat, Pete," John shouted. "You jump on board when I bring her alongside."

John manœuvred the boat close to the *Fulmar*. Peter gave a leap, swayed for a moment as if he was

6 81 (G 781)

going to fall back into the water, and then was seized in Mr. Baxter's powerful grip.

" There's a time bomb on board," shouted Peter.

It was one of Uncle George's many excellent qualities that when a nephew, who he thought was peacefully at home getting ready to go back to school, suddenly leapt on board wearing handcuffs and shouted that there was a time bomb on board, he did not waste time asking unnecessary questions.

" Where?" he said.

" I don't know. It was put on board last night."

Uncle George and Mr. Baxter looked at one another in a questioning manner. Then Mr. Baxter grunted, " That packing-case," and dived down the hatch to the motor.

He emerged carrying a wooden packing-case. He staggered to the side and threw it overboard.

" I thought it was those engine spares we ordered," he said.

Whether the warning had arrived on the nick of time or whether the internal mechanism of the bomb disliked its violent treatment at Mr. Baxter's hands can never be known. A bare minute after the packing-case had gone overboard a shower of spray shot into the air, followed after a second by a column of muddy water. The *Fulmar* shuddered with the shock of the explosion and the falling water splashed her deck.

" Gosh!" said Peter.

" Perhaps," said Uncle George in a conversational tone of voice, " you might give us some slight idea of what has been happening since we left you."

Peter gave him a brief account of their adventures. Uncle George muttered under his breath when Peter came to the part where Miss Stiggins showed her true colours. Apart from this and a couple of short questions, he did not interrupt Peter's story. But as soon as he had finished, Uncle George began issuing his orders.

"We'll anchor and I'll go ashore with John in the dinghy. Baxter, you remain on board to bring the *Fulmar* back to The Haven, towing the dinghy. You'll have to come ashore with us to sail the dinghy back. Peter, remain here till Baxter has removed your handcuffs."

He waved to the dinghy, which had been tacking to and fro near the yacht. In a minute Peter was alone on board.

In Mr. Baxter's skilful hands the dinghy beat up to the northern shore. He took her close to a rock with deep water alongside; Uncle George and John leapt on to the rock and the dinghy headed back to the yacht.

"We'll make for the lighthouse," said Uncle George. "That'll be the nearest telephone." And he started climbing up the cliff.

The next twenty minutes were much too strenuous for conversation. Uncle George went up the cliff at a tremendous pace. At the top he set off at a sort of lope. It looked restful, but John found himself running quite hard to keep up. Uncle George might be getting on for fifty but he certainly was remarkably fit.

When they reached the lighthouse Uncle George

went inside. John was very glad to throw himself on the grass to get his breath back.

As soon as he was recovered he followed Uncle George into the lighthouse. He found him telephoning hard, speaking in short staccato sentences. Two of the lighthouse-keepers were there. They nodded to John.

" Come on, young 'un," said one. " You're borrowing my motor bike. Give me a hand to get it out."

A moment later Uncle George joined them. He got on to the motor bicycle; John leapt on to the carrier; and they roared off in a cloud of dust and smoke.

" Where are we going?" John shouted.

" Ivy Cottage. The police ought to be there before us," Uncle George shouted back.

They were going at the maximum speed of which the bicycle was capable. Fortunately this was not very great, for, as they proceeded, John realized that motor bicycling was not one of Uncle George's accomplishments. To get to Ivy Cottage they had to go through Barton. In the traffic and the narrow streets their progress consisted of a series of shattering jerks. John felt as if he was riding a bucking bronco.

" Sorry," remarked Uncle George as John scrambled back on to the carrier, from which one of the jerks had nearly dislodged him. " It's fifteen years since I rode one of these things, and they seem to have to altered the control arrangements a bit."

Once clear of Barton, they made better progress.

They were still some distance from Ivy Cottage when they heard the unmistakable sharp crack of a rifle shot. It was followed by several more and then silence. Uncle George did not say anything, but John felt his muscles tauten for a second and knew that he had heard.

Two hundred yards from the cottage some police cars were parked by the side of the road. A policeman stepped out into the road and held up his hand. Uncle George explained who he was and they were allowed to proceed.

The atmosphere of deep rural peace which normally surrounded Ivy Cottage had departed. The front door hung drunkenly where it had been broken down. The house and garden were full of policemen, some of whom were carrying rifles.

If the outside of the cottage was changed, the alteration in the sitting-room was even more startling. One of the windows was completely shattered by the police rifle fire. The curtains blew about wildly in the wind. The floor was littered with broken china; the wall opposite the window was pitted with marks of bullets. A policeman was sitting in a chair, having a wound in his shoulder dressed.

It was only after he had taken all this in that John noticed something in the corner by the spinning-wheel. It was roughly covered by a rug. From one edge of the rug a foot projected, a foot which he recognized by the shoe as belonging to Miss Stiggins.

Uncle George was talking to an Inspector of Police who seemed to know him.

"Just as well you warned us that they were armed," the inspector was saying. "She opened fire as soon as we appeared. Crack shot she was too. Several of us had narrow squeaks. Luckily Simpson here was the only one hit and his shoulder is not too bad."

"What about the man?" Uncle George asked.

"They're searching the house and grounds now. I expect he's away, though. She would be covering his retreat as long as possible. Funny thing, her name really was Miss Stiggins. Apparently she had lived a quiet respectable life for years. Wonder how she got mixed up in this racket. She certainly had guts."

At this point a sergeant entered. "We've been right through the house and grounds, sir. There's no one hidden there," he reported.

"Right," said the inspector. "Now, young man," turning to John, "describe this fellow as accurately as you can."

John described Vassili to the best of his ability, while a constable took down the description in shorthand in his notebook.

"Good," the inspector said. "We'll get that circulated. They should be having all the roads and railway watched. I'll get back and check up on it."

Uncle George pointed to the telephone, which had received a direct hit from a bullet. "I must telephone but I don't think I'll get much result from this instrument. Can you give me a lift into Barton?"

The police cars had been full when they arrived. By the time Uncle George and the wounded policeman had got in there was obviously no room for

John. The only thing left seemed to be to go back to The Haven. A single policeman had been left to guard Ivy Cottage, and John re-entered to tell him where he was going.

He had barely started speaking when there was the sound of someone running. They stopped and turned towards the door just in time to see Peter, minus his handcuffs at last, burst into the room.

" Gosh!" said Peter.

" How on earth did you get here?" John asked.

" After he had got rid of my handcuffs, Mr. Baxter put me ashore. He said that he could manage the boats himself and that I might as well be in at the finish. What's happened?"

John explained. Peter looked round the room, noting the signs of battle.

Suddenly he cried: " The sewing-machine! The one she got so cross about when you wanted to touch it; it's gone." John looked round the room. Peter was right. There was no sign of the new-looking sewing-machine. " Vassili must have taken it," Peter continued. " It must be the lead container for the Iconium."

It was Peter who had the flashes of inspiration, but John who had to do the serious planning. Now he began thinking furiously.

" It must be very heavy," he said slowly. " If Vassili has taken it with him, he must hope to escape. They said he would take us with him, so there must be a boat coming in to-night somewhere near here. Sandy Cove! We must warn them."

The policeman had been following this conver-

sation with some bewilderment. Now he broke in:
" If you want to warn anyone, you'll have to go
to Barton. I can't leave here."

" The motor bike," cried John.

They rushed out to where Uncle George had
left the motor bicycle. The back tyre was flat.

" What about getting our bikes from The Haven
and going on them?" asked Peter.

" No good. There's not time. We must go straight
to Sandy Cove on our bikes and stop Vassili ourselves."

IT was getting dark by the time that the boys got back to The Haven and collected their bicycles.

" Do you realize that it is only three days ago since we helped Miss Stiggins with her flat tyre?" John asked.

" Seems like a week. I suppose she must have let the tyre down herself, so she could find out what we were doing."

" And then she must have gone on to Barton Church to leave the message for Vassili in the Bible. No wonder she told us not to wait for her."

Just beyond Ivy Cottage a track led off the road to the right, running along the top of the Pottles towards Sandy Cove. It was the track along which Peter had come after being landed.

" You lead, Pete. You know the way."

" I hope so. It's going to be rather tricky in this light."

" Well, we've got to do it, if we're going to catch Vassili."

It certainly was tricky riding a bicycle along the track. It was in many ways a repetition of their ride on the moor when they were following Professor Ksk. Luckily the track in this case was fairly flat, but in the fading light it needed great concentration. In the haste of their departure they had not waited to ship their headlamps, which did not help matters.

"I wish I'd asked for a dynamo set last Christmas," puffed John.

Peter regained the track with an effort, just avoiding a protruding gorse bush. "You think the police will charge us for riding without lights, if we find them?" he asked frivolously.

It was after they had passed the Pottles and were on the rougher ground of the moor that disaster overtook them. Going too fast downhill, Peter hit a stone, shot across the road into a boulder and went over the handlebars. John, in trying to avoid him, went off the other side of the track over a drop into a stream. Neither of them was much hurt, but Peter's front wheel was bent into a graceful curve and John's bicycle was not in much better state.

"We'll have to push on on foot," said John, wiping some of the mud from his face.

Sandy Cove was still a mile away but they set off half running and half walking. Suddenly Peter shouted: "Look! On top of the ridge."

John stopped and looked. Silhouetted against the sky was a man. He was thickset with a bullet head: he was carrying something: he was moving at a shambling bear-like trot. Even at that distance there was no mistaking him. It was Vassili.

" Quick, we must cut him off!" cried John.

The track they had been following was turning inland, but in the half light they could make out a footpath running off to the right along the cliffs, which now bordered the river. Along this they dashed. They could no longer make out Vassili, now that he had left the skyline.

Both boys had had a remarkably strenuous day, but the last half mile to Sandy Cove was covered at a pace which would have been creditable on a track. At last they topped a rise and Sandy Cove lay open before them. The beach was deserted, but in the bay, close to the beach, lay a low, dark motor boat.

A moment later they saw Vassili. He was barely two hundred yards away, but he might as well have been two hundred miles. It was clear now why the track had turned inland. Between them and Vassili ran a great cleft nearly quarter of a mile long. To make things worse, they could see that Peter had been right. Vassili was carrying the sewing-machine hung by a strap. It seemed that they would merely be helpless spectators of Vassili's escape.

Then John saw another thing. Not far from the path down which Vassili was making his way to the beach was a tent. It was in a hollow and difficult to see against the dark background. In front of the tent was a slender wireless aerial.

" Professor! Professor! Stop him! He's a thief!" John shouted.

Vassili did stop momentarily, seeing the boys for the first time. Then he continued on his way. But Peter now joined John shouting. They saw the flaps of the tent open and a great black-bearded head emerge. Vassili also saw and shouted something threatening in his own language.

The effect on Professor Ksk was the opposite of what Vassili must have expected. He gave a roar of rage and hurled himself on Vassili. The opponents were not unevenly matched. Vassili was the younger, but the Professor's simian form showed his immense strength.

The boys could see the men locked together in a tremendous struggle, but by now it was too dark to see clearly. Also they had no time for being mere spectators. As soon as the two men grappled, the boys began racing round the cleft to the Professor's assistance.

But they were not the only reinforcements. Out of the corner of his eye John saw two men jump out of the motor boat and begin wading ashore. This would more than redress the balance in Vassili's favour. The only hope was to knock out Vassili before his friends could join him, though this seemed a faint chance.

As the boys rounded the end of the cleft and began running towards the Professor, they could only make out a vaguely struggling mass on the ground. Then all at once they could see quite clearly. The headlights of a car had come over the ridge.

They saw Vassili break away, stagger to his feet and start running for the beach. Professor Ksk also got up and began to follow, but after a few yards he stopped. By the time the boys reached him he was puffing and blowing like a decrepit steam-engine.

"Ach, I am too old to run," he gasped. "Zese men, zey drove me from my country. They are——"
Here the Professor's English was inadequate to express his own feelings, and he uttered some explosive-sounding word in his own tongue.

There was no point in following Vassili. He had reached the water's edge and was wading out to the motor boat. The crew had started the engine: two men hauled Vassili on board: the motor boat roared out to sea, just as a jeep, skidding with locked wheels, drew up alongside the boys. Uncle George and two policemen jumped out.

"The sewing-machine," cried Peter.

There, lying where Vassili had dropped it, and clearly illuminated in the headlights of the jeep, lay Miss Stiggins's sewing-machine. Peter tried to pick it up. He could barely move it. It felt like lead. The search for the missing Iconium was finished.

"It wasn't until we got to Barton that I realized that this cove wasn't being watched," Uncle George's cool voice said. "Luckily we got here just in time."

"But you're just too late," John broke in. "Vassili's escaped."

Uncle George pointed out to sea. The boys looked and saw a pencil of white light, then another and another.

"I got on to the Naval Commander-in-Chief from the lighthouse. He sent out a flotilla of motor gunboats. They can do forty knots easily. If they don't pick up the motor boat with their search-lights, they will with their radar. I don't think you need worry about Vassili."

Uncle George was interrupted by Professor Ksk's hand being laid on his shoulder.

"George," said the Professor, "zese are very strange birds zat you and your young friends go vatching."